The Bringers of Wetherton Bee

Written by Amanda Redstone &

illustrated by Genevieve Lowles

GINGERBELL BOOKS

There once was a village called Wetherton Bee,
Where bringernooks lived in small huts in a tree.
And there they all bumbled and bimbled around,
Perched happily forty feet high from the ground.

3

Now if you've not met any bringernooks yet,
I'll tell you at once while the ink is still wet.

They're small and they're bustling with braids in their hair,
And beards that curl up whenever they're scared.

5

They keep to themselves and they don't like to travel,
And when they're contented, their beards unravel.
You'll see if you look at the beard of a 'nook,
Their tags rustle softly like pages of books.

Each tag is a memory or something they've done,
Or a story they've heard or a song that they've sung,

Or a joke that they've told or a place where they've been,
Or a 'nook that they've met, or a smile that they've seen.

In Wetherton Bee all the tags that they grow,
Are yellow and blue when the beards are on show.

And though they are cheerful and bright to behold,
The colours all match from the young to the old.

Introduction

One night as young Tibin sat down to have tea,
The 'nook heard a knocking and went out to see.

The sight there before him befuddled his head,
A strange sort of 'nook who'd come knocking for bread.

The visitor stood on the bringernook's porch,
Her marvellous beard was lit up by her torch;
Her colourful tags were quite brazenly showing;
The reds, greens and purples were vibrantly glowing.

"Hello," said the 'nook with a confident smile,
"Excuse all the mud, I've been walking for miles."
"Would you happen to have," Rai politely enquired,
"A small snack and a bed, for I'm ever so tired?"

Shy Tibin stared rudely, his eyes growing wide,
Uncertain if he should invite her inside.
His beard curled up as his fear overtook,
For never before had he seen such a 'nook.

Her tags told of places befitting a dream –
Of creatures and beasts that he never had seen.
Her eyes shone like rock pools bewitched by a spell,
Alive with adventure and stories to tell.

When intrigue defeated the bringernook's fright,
He graciously offered a bed for the night.
He sat his new guest in his comfiest chair,
And brought out the last of his dinner to share.

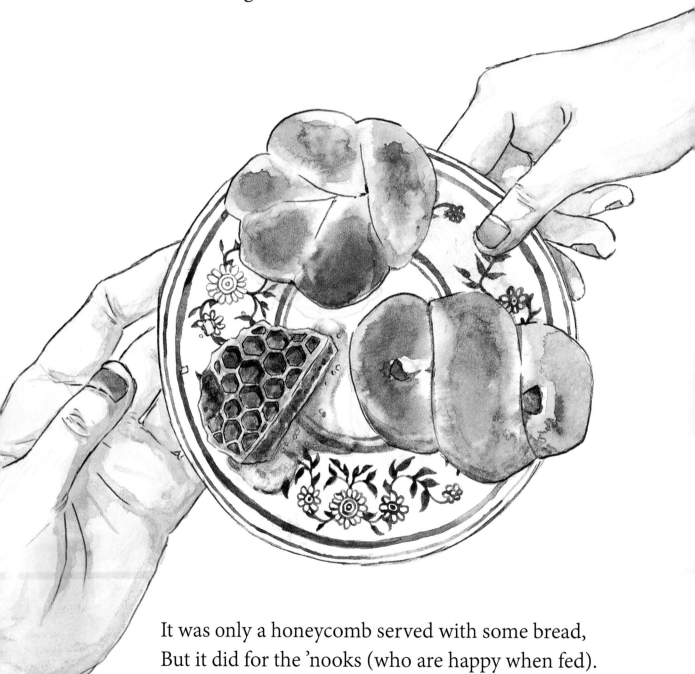

It was only a honeycomb served with some bread,
But it did for the 'nooks (who are happy when fed).

They sat by the fire and basked in its heat,
Two 'nooks swapping stories and warming their feet.

As each of Rai's stories began to unfurl,
Our nervous 'nook's beard began to uncurl,
Where once there had been only yellow and blue,
A sprinkling of green now began to shine through.

And Tibin could see as he studied his friend,
Her beard now had flecks of bright blue at the ends.

He thought to himself as he went off to bed:
It suited her well as it mixed with the red.

When the sun nudged the 'nook from his sleep with its light,
He began to remember the previous night.
"Was it something I dreamt?" he started to think,
'Til he caught his reflection above the small sink.

His beard had curled up like a hedgehog in terror,
But slowly relaxed as he looked in the mirror.
He felt somehow wiser and just a bit bold
In breaking away from his comfortable mould.

With fizzing excitement inflating his chest
The 'nook prepared breakfast for him and his guest.

His beard bobbing gently below his round chin,
He thought of adventures about to begin.

Draw yourself as a Bringernook!

My name is

....